Hansel and Gretel

Hansel and Gretel

by the BROTHERS GRIMM

illustrated by
PAUL GALDONE

McGRAW-HILL BOOK COMPANY
New York   St. Louis   San Francisco

For

Barbara, Steven

Tanya, and Travis

1 2 3 4 5 6 7 8 9 RABP 8 7 6 5 4 3 2

LIBRARY OF CONGRESS CATALOGING IN PUBLICATION DATA

GALDONE, Paul

Hänsel und Gretel. English.

   Hansel and Gretel.

   Translation of : Hänsel und Gretel.

   Summary: A poor woodcutter's two children, lost
in the woods, come upon a gingerbread house inhabited
by a wicked witch.

  [1. Fairy tales. 2. Folklore—Germany] 1. Grimm,
Jakob, 1785–1863. Hansel und Gretel. II. Galdone,
Paul, ill. III. Title.

PZ8.H196 1982   398.2'1'0943 [E]   82-9979

ISBN 0-07-022727-6   PT   AACR2

Close to a large forest there lived a woodcutter with his wife and his two children. The boy was called Hansel and the girl Gretel. They were always very poor and had very little to live on. And at one time when there was famine in the land, the father could no longer provide for them.

One night when he lay in bed worrying over his troubles, he sighed and said to his wife, "What is to become of us? How are we to feed our poor children when we have nothing for ourselves?"

"I'll tell you what, husband," answered the woman, who was not the children's mother. "Tomorrow morning we will take the children out quite early into the thickest part of the forest. We will light a fire and give each of them a piece of bread. Then we will go to our work and leave them alone. They won't be able to find their way back, and so we shall be rid of them."

"Nay, wife," said the man, "we won't do that. I could never find it in my heart to leave my children alone in the forest. Wild animals would soon tear them to pieces."

"What a fool you are!" she said. "Then we must all four die of hunger."

She gave him no peace till he consented. "But I grieve over the poor children all the same," said the man.

The two children could not go to sleep for hunger either, and they heard what their stepmother said to their father.

Gretel wept bitterly and said, "All is over with us now."

"Be quiet, Gretel," said Hansel. "Don't cry! I will find some way out of it."

When the old people had gone to sleep, he got up, put on his little coat, opened the door, and slipped out. The moon was shining brightly and the white pebbles around the house shone like newly minted coins.

Hansel stooped down and put as many into his pockets as they would hold.

Then he went back to Gretel and said, "Take comfort, little sister, and go to sleep. God won't forsake us." And then he went to bed again.

At daybreak, before the sun had risen, the woman came and said, "Get up, you lazybones! We are going into the forest to fetch wood."

Then she gave them each a piece of bread and said, "Here is something for your dinner, but don't eat it before then, for you'll get no more."

Gretel put the bread under her apron, for Hansel had the stones in his pockets. Then they all started for the forest. When they had gone a little way, Hansel stopped and looked back at the cottage, and he did the same thing again and again.

His father said, "Hansel, what are you stopping to look back at? Take care and put your best foot foremost."

"Oh, father," said Hansel, "I am looking at my white cat. It is sitting on the roof, wanting to say good-by to me."

"Little fool, that's no cat! It's the morning sun shining on the chimney," said the woman.

But Hansel had not been looking at the cat. He had dropped a pebble on the ground each time he stopped.

When they reached the middle of the forest, their father said, "Now, children, pick up some wood. I want to make a fire to warm you."

Hansel and Gretel gathered the twigs together and soon made a huge pile. Then the pile was lighted, and when it blazed up the woman said, "Now lie down by the fire and rest yourselves while we go and cut wood. When we have finished we will come back to fetch you."

Hansel and Gretel sat by the fire, and when dinnertime came they each ate their little bit of bread, and they thought their father was quite near because they could hear the sound of an ax. It was no ax, however, but a branch which the man had tied to a dead tree, and which blew backwards and forwards against it. They sat there so long a time that they got tired. Then their eyes began to close and they were soon fast asleep.

When they woke it was dark night. Gretel began to cry, "How shall we ever get out of the wood?"

But Hansel comforted her and said, "Wait a little while till the moon rises, and then we will find our way."

When the full moon rose, Hansel took his little sister's hand and they walked on, guided by the pebbles, which glittered like newly coined money. They walked the whole night, and at daybreak they found themselves back at their father's cottage.

They knocked at the door, and when the woman opened it and saw Hansel and Gretel she said, "You bad children, why did you sleep so long in the wood? We thought you did not mean to come back any more."

But their father was delighted, for it had gone to his heart to leave them behind alone.

Not long afterwards the children heard the woman at night in bed say to their father, "We have eaten up everything again but half a loaf, and then we will be at the end of everything. The children must go away! We will take them farther into the forest so that they won't be able to find their way back. There is nothing else to be done."

The man took it much to heart and said, "We had better share our last crust with the children."

But the woman would not listen to a word he said. She only scolded and reproached him. As the father had given in the first time he had to do so the second. The children were again wide awake and heard what was said.

When the old people went to sleep Hansel again got up, meaning to go out and get some more pebbles, but the woman had locked the door and he couldn't get out. But he consoled his little sister and said, "Don't cry, Gretel. Go to sleep. God will help us."

In the early morning the woman made the children get up and gave them each a piece of bread, but it was smaller than the last. On the way to the forest Hansel crumbled it up in his pocket, and stopped every now and then to throw a crumb onto the ground.

"Hansel, what are you stopping to look about you for?" asked his father.

"I am looking at my dove, which is sitting on the roof and wants to say good-by to me," answered Hansel.

"Little fool," said the woman, "that is no dove! It is the morning sun shining on the chimney."

Nevertheless, Hansel strewed the crumbs from time to time on the ground. The woman led the children far into the forest, where they had never been before.

Again they made a big fire, and the woman said, "Stay where you are, children, and when you are tired you may go to sleep for a while. We are going farther on to cut wood, and in the evening when we have finished we will come back and fetch you."

At dinnertime Gretel shared her bread with Hansel, for he had crumbled his upon the road. Then they went to sleep and the evening passed, but no one came to fetch the poor children.

It was quite dark when they woke up, and Hansel cheered his little sister. He said, "Wait a bit, Gretel, till the moon rises, and then we can see the bread crumbs which I scattered to show us the way home."

When the moon rose they started, but they found no bread crumbs, for the birds in the forest had picked them up and eaten them.

Hansel said to Gretel, "We shall soon find the way." But they could not find it. They walked the whole night and all the next day from morning till night, but they could not get out of the forest.

They were very hungry, for they had nothing to eat but a few berries that they found. They were so tired that their legs would not carry them any farther, and they lay down under a tree and went to sleep.

When they woke in the morning, it was the third day since they had left their father's cottage. They started to walk again, but they only got deeper and deeper into the wood.

At midday they saw a beautiful snow-white bird sitting on a tree. It sang so beautifully that they stood still to listen to it. When it stopped, it fluttered its wings and flew around them. They followed it until they came to a little cottage, where it settled on the roof.

When they got quite near, they saw that the little house
was made of gingerbread and roofed with cakes. The windows
were transparent sugar.

"Here is something for us," said Hansel. "We will have a good meal. I will have a piece of the roof, Gretel, and you can have a bit of the window. It will be nice and sweet."

Hansel reached up and broke off a piece of the roof to see what it tasted like. Gretel went to the window and nibbled at that. A gentle voice called out from within:

> *"Nibbling, nibbling like a mouse,*
> *Who's nibbling at my little house?"*

The children answered:

> *"The wind, the wind doth blow*
> *From heaven to earth below."*

And they went on eating without disturbing themselves.

Hansel, who found the roof very good, broke off a large piece for himself, and Gretel pushed a whole round pane out of the window and started to enjoy it.

All at once the door opened and an old, old woman, supporting herself on a crutch, came hobbling out. Hansel and Gretel were so frightened that they dropped what they held in their hands.

But the old woman only shook her head and said, "Ah, dear children, who brought you here? Come in and stay with me. You will come to no harm."

She took them by the hand and led them into the little house. A nice dinner was set before them: pancakes and sugar, milk, apples, and nuts. After this she showed them two little white beds into which they snuggled, and they felt as if they were in heaven.

Although the old woman appeared to be so friendly, she was really a wicked old witch who was on the watch for children, and she had built the gingerbread house on purpose to lure them to her. Whenever she could get a child into her clutches she cooked it and considered it a grand feast.

When Hansel and Gretel came near her, she laughed wickedly to herself and said scornfully, "Now that I have them, they shan't escape me."

She got up early in the morning before the children were awake, and when she saw them sleeping, with their beautiful rosy cheeks, she murmured to herself, "They will be dainty morsels."

She seized Hansel with her bony hand and dragged him off to a shed, where she locked him up behind a barred door. He screamed as loud as he could but she took no notice of him.

Then she went to Gretel and shook her till she woke, and cried, "Get up, little lazybones! Fetch some water and cook something nice for your brother. He is in the shed and has to be fattened. When he is nice and fat, I will eat him."

Gretel began to cry bitterly, but it was no use; she had to obey the witch's orders. The best food was cooked for poor Hansel, but Gretel had only the shells of crayfish.

The old woman hobbled to the shed every morning and cried, "Hansel, put your finger out for me to feel how fat you are."

Hansel put out a knucklebone, and the old woman, whose eyes were too dim to see, thought it was his finger. And she was much astonished that he did not get fat.

When four weeks had passed and Hansel still kept thin, she became impatient and would wait no longer.

"Now then, Gretel," she cried, "bustle along and fetch the water. Fat or thin, I will cook Hansel and eat him."

Oh, how his poor little sister grieved! As she carried the water, the tears streamed down her cheeks. "Dear God, help us!" she cried.

"You may spare your lamentations! They will do you no good," said the old woman.

Early in the morning Gretel had to go out to fill the kettle with water, and then she had to kindle a fire and hang the kettle over it.

"We will bake first," said the old witch. "I have heated the oven and kneaded the dough."

She pushed poor Gretel towards the oven and said, "Creep in and see if it is properly heated, and then we will put the bread in."

She meant, when Gretel had gone in, to shut the door and roast her, but Gretel saw her intention and said, "I don't know how to get in. How am I to manage it?"

"Silly goose!" cried the witch. "The opening is big enough. You can see that I could get into it myself."

She hobbled up and stuck her head into the oven. But Gretel pushed the witch right in, and then she banged the door shut and bolted it.

Then Gretel ran away and left the wicked witch to perish miserably.

Gretel ran as fast as she could to the shed. She opened the door and cried, "Hansel, we are saved! The old witch is dead."

Hansel sprang out, like a bird out of a cage when the door is set open. How delighted they were. They hugged and kissed each other and danced about for joy.

As they had nothing more to fear, they went into the witch's house, and in every corner they found chests full of pearls and precious stones.

"These are better than pebbles," said Hansel, as he filled his pockets.

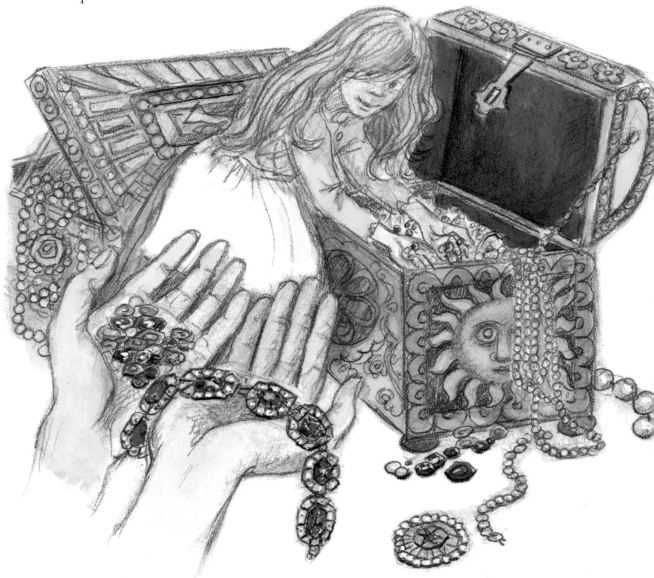

Gretel said, "I must take something home with me too." And she filled her apron.

"But now we must go," said Hansel, "so that we may get out of this enchanted wood."

Before they had gone very far, they came to a pond.

"We can't get across it," said Hansel. "I see no stepping stones and no bridge."

"And there are no boats either," answered Gretel, "but there is a duck swimming. It will help us over if we ask it."

So she cried:

> *"Little duck that cries quack, quack,*
> *Here Gretel and here Hansel stand.*
> *Quickly take us on your back,*
> *No path nor bridge is there at hand!"*

The duck came swimming towards them, and Hansel got on its back and told his sister to sit on his knee.

"No," answered Gretel, "it will be too heavy for the duck. It must take us over one after the other."

The good creature did this, and when they had got safely over and walked for a while the woods seemed to grow more and more familiar to them, and at last they saw their father's cottage in the distance.

They began to run, and rushed inside, where they threw their arms around their father's neck. The man had not had a single happy moment since he deserted his children in the forest, and in the meantime his wife had died.

Gretel shook her apron and scattered the pearls and precious stones all over the floor, and Hansel added handful after handful out of his pockets.

So all their troubles came to an end, and they lived together as happily as possible.